The Worrying WORRIES

RACHEL ROONEY   ZEHRA HICKS

ANDERSEN PRESS

Once, I found a Worry so I trapped it in a net.

I picked it out and put it in my pocket for a pet.

Everywhere I went that day, my Worry came with me.

The library...

the shops...

the park...

and home again for tea.

It soon became a nuisance.

It tangled up my hair.

It tugged my sleeve.

It itched my skin.

It stole my favourite chair.

I pushed away my pasta.

I couldn't eat my cake.

I lost my appetite because
I'd got a stomach ache.

But Worries have a hunger.
They feed upon your fears.

It nibbled on my
fingernails...

and sipped my salty tears.

It whispered mean words in my ear.

Put sad thoughts in my head.

It followed me upstairs...

... and hogged the duvet on my bed.

It fidgeted and wiggled.

It met me in my sleep.

When I woke I knew it was a pet I couldn't keep.

I'd had enough of worrying.
I took my Worry pet
to see a Worry Expert.

(She was once a Worry Vet.)

I told her what the matter was.
She nodded once or twice.
She rubbed her chin and thought a bit.
Then offered this advice...

A Worry is an awful pest but it won't do you harm.
Try these simple exercises. They will keep you calm.

We practised painting
pictures in our head.

We shut our eyes.
And thought of

sunshine...

seasides...

flowers...

ice cream...

butterflies.

We practised statue-standing.

Kept as still as we could be.

Breathing slowly in and out while counting...

One...

Two...

Three.

We practised squeezing muscles tighter than a mother's hug.

Then made our bodies floppy like a jelly or a slug.

Keep practising, the expert said.
Your day has just begun.

Now you need to leave and
practise having lots of fun...

I followed her instructions...

It seemed to do the trick.

I haven't seen the Worry since.

Now I'm not worried sick.